# Sally
## AND THE
# Some-Thing

## GEORGE O'CONNOR

A NEAL PORTER BOOK
ROARING BROOK PRESS
NEW MILFORD, CONNECTICUT

*Arta Khanoom. My heart.*
*I love you this much.*

*Special thanks*
*to Kevin Lewis.*

Copyright © 2006 by George O'Connor

Published by Roaring Brook Press

Roaring Brook Press is a division of Holtzbrinck

Publishing Holdings Limited Partnership

143 West Street, New Milford, Connecticut 06776

Distributed in Canada by H. B. Fenn and Company Ltd.

Library of Congress Cataloging-in-Publication Data

O'Connor, George.

Sally and the Some-Thing / by George O'Connor.— 1st ed.

p. cm.

"A Neal Porter book."

Summary: One boring day, Sally goes down to the pond where

she meets a new friend who is really something.

ISBN-13: 978-1-59643-141-6

ISBN-10: 1-59643-141-5

[1. Monsters—Fiction. 2. Friendship—Fiction.]

I. Title: Sally and the Something.  II. Title.

PZ7.O22185Sal 2006

[E]—dc22

2005017326

Roaring Brook Press books are available for special promotions and premiums.

For details contact: Director of Special Markets, Holtzbrinck Publishers.

First Edition April 2006

Printed in the United States of America

10  9  8  7  6  5  4  3  2  1

"This place is boring," Sally said. "I'm going to the pond to catch something."

"Be back in time for dinner," said Sally's mom.

And so, with her fishing pole and tackle box she went

past the big mud puddle . . .

. . . she reached the pond.
Sally cast out her fishing line and waited . . .

and waited . . .

and waited . . .

After awhile, she realized that something was watching her.

Then something **sli-i-i-ithered.**

Something **slu-u-u-urped**.

"I don't know *what* you are,"
Sally told the Some-Thing.
"But I know you're not
boring! Let's go play."

But the Some-Thing
wasn't very good
with crayons.

The tea party
was a disaster.

And the less said about
the bicycle, the better.

"That didn't go so well," said Sally. "Maybe we should try some of *your* favorite things."

the Some-Thing agreed.

But Sally didn't appreciate
the Some-Thing's collection.

The snail races
were a real snooze.

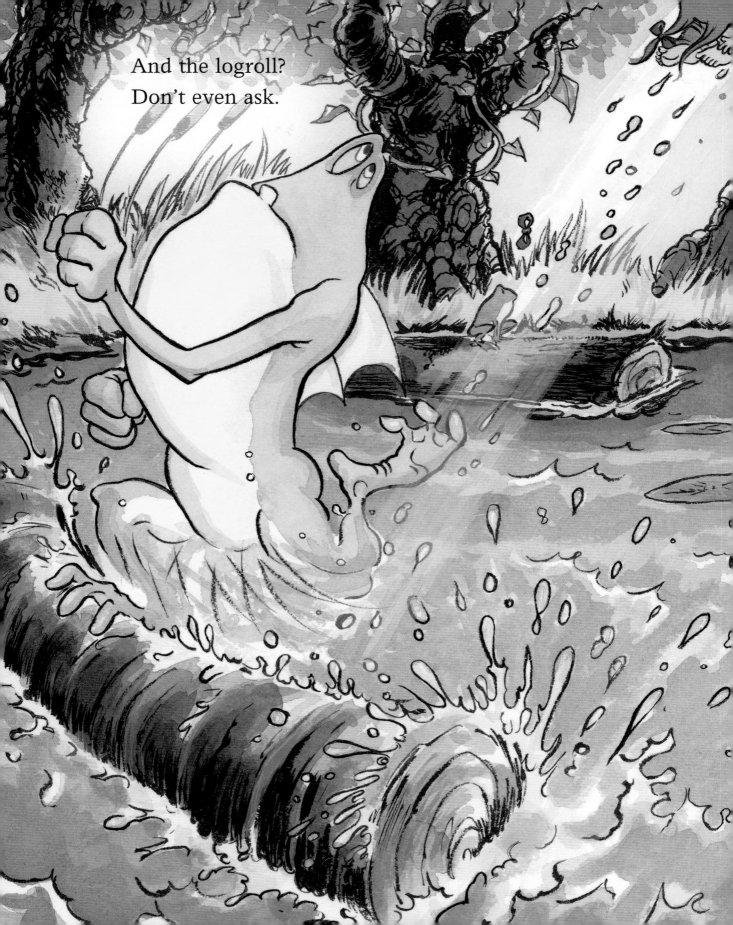

And the logroll?
Don't even ask.

# BLIPPITY-BLOOP?

asked the Some-Thing.

"That went worse than expected," said Sally. "Maybe we should make up some *new* games for us to play together."

So here's what they did.

They had a burping contest (Sally won).

They played leapfrog
(the Some-Thing was a natural).

And Sally made
the best mudpies the
Some-Thing had
ever tasted.

"The secret is in the
mud," said Sally.

They played on and on and on.

Eventually,
the Some-Thing
got tired.

"You can hardly keep your eyes open,"
said Sally. "Let's get you home."

By the time Sally
reached home it
was almost dark.

"Catch anything?" her mom asked. "No, but I met a friend," said Sally.

"Really? What's your new friend like?" Sally's mom asked.

"Well," said Sally.
"He's really something."